The
Curious
Mind

Raymond H. Whitelockecrawford

The Curious Mind
A Whitelockecrawford Book/May 2014

Cover Photo by Jacob Gminski
Cover Design by Jennifer Baldwin and Raymond H.
Whitelockecrawford

Printed in the United States by Createspace, an Amazon
Company

ISBN 9781481291361

First Edition

Thanks

Mary Whitelockecrawford

Gianna Gminski

Preface

The mind has a profound effect on one's ability to render with confidence the tasks one imagines, be they small and everyday, or be they some of the greatest undertakings humanity has ever seen. From getting up in the morning, preparing to face the day ahead, to work that will win Nobel Prizes, and from the kindergarten student learning to tie a shoe to the philosophers of ancient days, it is the mind that allows each person to do what he or she has set out to do. It is the mind, more than almost any other factor that can lead one to success.

The human mind is innately curious: we always want to learn more. This fundamental truth of the human condition has led society to where it is today, as people have striven again and again to improve themselves, their situations, and their technology, and to understand the world around them. This curiosity, and the accompanying urge to better ourselves, is a huge part of what separates humanity from the animals, such as the apes to which we are so closely related.

But how do we harness and manage this curiosity? All people have a certain amount of it, but our most successful thinkers, leaders, and luminaries must have something special about the way they use that most powerful of human tools, the mind. Influenced by education, culture, upbringing, and a plethora of other factors, those who make names for themselves are often those who use their minds uniquely and most effectively. To understand what made Caesar a great leader, what made Steve Jobs or Bill Gates such innovative thinkers, what engendered the strategic genius of General Patton or Colin Powell: such quest has interested many. The following is my exploration of some of the most fascinating aspects relating to the will of the mind.

Chapter One

Different minds have different strengths and weaknesses, which ultimately lead them down different paths and cause them to influence society in different ways. Imagine that there was only one sort of great mind—one variety of thinkers acknowledged as the best and most effective. Surely our society would suffer, since different types of thinkers and different minds are suited to different professions and lines of work, this then means that if we had only one type of thinker, we would not have come nearly as far as we have as a society.

Imagine if Bill Clinton's childhood diplomatic inklings had been squashed and that he had instead been encouraged to go into the sciences or a discipline for which he had no interest and no special ability. What a great loss it would have been! This is not to say that Clinton would not have made an outstanding scientist who made great contributions; rather, the point is that his unique genius, which involves charming people, bringing them together, and helping them to reach common ground, might not have found its full expression in a scientific milieu.

On the flip side of the same coin, forcing a great scientific mind, like that of Albert Einstein, into the modes of thought common to politicians would have been a disaster. An awkward man who did not read until the age of eight or even speak until age three, Einstein would have been a failure in this discipline, and the world would likely have been poorer as a result, for, though relativity might have been discovered without Einstein, it was his particular mind that brought it to light according to his own unique way.

Entertainers, it is clear, have talent—a combination of the mental and physical performance that is worthy of its own exploration. However, much of it comes from the mind. When Beethoven, who could not even hear the music he composed, understood it through vibrations that was a function of his mind. Like Mozart, who wrote his first sonata at the age of three and his first symphony at seven,

Beethoven was a genius that was more mental than physical. These two men had minds that simply worked differently from those of other people, or even other musicians and composers. In fact, their brains were even quite different from each other.

The fact that all of these great men's mental processes led them toward their individual fields, though, was more than chance, and, indeed, more than simple aptitude for one area of study or another. All of these people were passionate about their work and wanted to use their talents, enduring difficult times—and in the case of Caesar, even sacrificing life itself—to do so. This, then, is another dimension of what the mind can do. It can and does create desire, serving as an instrument to push people toward the disciplines they eventually go into. So often, it seems, the discipline one chooses is that for which a mind is best suited: Winston Churchill, for example, as the son of a privileged family, had many paths open to him. He was irresistibly drawn toward politics, and the world is different—and likely better—as a result.

The combination of special talent and the desire to go into a profession where it can best be used is almost mystical. So many factors go into the workings of even the most pedestrian mind— the characters examined herein are much more than that. Clearly, there are a myriad of forces at work within the mind.

One of the factors at work in the mind of any individual is his or her thoughts: wants, desires, and plans that help shape any person's actions. Although these thoughts are such a factor, they can in turn be influenced by a wide range of things. For instance, when one wakes up in the morning and has slept badly, the first thoughts one has are probably of nothing more notable than returning to sleep, but even as one awakens further and goes about the business of the day, thoughts may be retarded, coming slowly and sluggishly because of a lack of sleep.

Even something as seemingly insignificant as the time of day can influence thoughts: at certain times of the day, thoughts of even the most dedicated thinker turn to food, for example. We all must eat to sustain ourselves, but for some, thoughts about it get in the way of other, more productive uses of the mind, especially if food is not readily available.

Another factor that influences one's mind is the consideration of the perspective of others. Some people are fearless, able to forge their own paths no matter what disapproval or even despair they may leave in their wake. William Shakespeare, one of the greatest authors of all time, left his wife and small children at home in the tiny village of Stratford-upon-Avon, moving to London to pursue his muse and write his plays and poetry. Clearly, he was not affected by the thought of family and their opinions, but if he had been, it is easy to see how we might have had far fewer of his amazing plays and poems, since considering them might have kept him from fully exercising his prodigious talent.

Many other sorts of thoughts can influence the otherwise curious, talented and energetic mind, but a final sort worth noting is that of the many everyday concerns of day-to-day living, which we have had with us since ancient times. Though the substance of these thoughts may change, they remain powerful. How to make enough money to have a roof over one's head, food on the table, and other necessities is, for some, an overwhelming concern. It is perhaps one of the world's great tragedies that we will never know what amazing minds might have been so consumed with these mundane thoughts that they never had the time to make great discoveries or engage in amazing flights of fancy. Perhaps some even died before their time for lack of these necessities, and their hypothetical contributions to the world of thought, inquiry, and scholarship were never made.

The ideas a person is exposed to are other factors in the work of the mind. Many great thinkers were schooled by others. The ideas they absorbed had a lot to do with their future work and contributions: one has only to look at Plato, student of Socrates, for a telling example of this point. Not all great thinkers, of course, were schooled by philosophers, and yet the schooling they received or ideas they were exposed to had an effect on their minds in most cases. Some were inspired by what they were taught to go directly against it. One such thinker was Galileo, who, schooled in the church, rejected its fundamental notion of the universe and was branded a heretic. Others expanded on what they had been taught or looked at it in a new way, building on the foundations of thinkers before them.

Beliefs are another crucial influence in the life of the mind. For much of human history, the church was the refuge of the educated, as well as the source of most or all education in the Western world. People who might have gone into other areas became religious thinkers because it was the best (or only) avenue for them to have any life of the mind at all. Beliefs also influenced the priorities of thinkers: architects, for example, expressed their genius in the Western world through churches for hundreds of years because of the strong role that Christian belief played in society and in what they had been taught. Ultimately, beliefs, along with the ideas to which culture exposes people, exert a strong pull on even the most inventive minds, combining with talent, disposition, and other factors to influence the contributions of each curious mind to the world and to its ever-growing body of knowledge.

What causes the spark of inspiration to strike? Philosophers have pondered the question at length, but for purposes of the exploration at hand, it matters less how inspiration comes and more what inspires each person, for it is this that shapes the mind's subsequent work. What inspires people varies greatly, but it has a lot to do with what people are exposed to and what they experience. Dancers, for example, are not inspired to dance a particular technique unless they know that kind of dance exists: without seeing, hearing about, or otherwise being aware of such dance, their inspiration to become practitioners of the art might never come.

Inspiration can also come from a problem set before someone. Inventors set out to solve problems—even Neanderthals and early *Homo sapiens* were doing that when they created stone tools. Problems that provide inspiration do not have to be of a physical nature; however. The courageous action and well-reasoned thought of Susan B. Anthony, Lucretia Mott, Elizabeth Cady Stanton, and other reformers for women's rights and for the abolition of slavery, for they were inspired by what they perceived to be social problems. Inspiration might come from other people with whom one interacts. Maurice Sendak, the brilliant, recently deceased writer of *Where the Wild Things Are,* was inspired to write the story of Max and his adventures with wild monsters by the experience of his own childhood. Feeling misunderstood by his parents and other adults, and characterized as a "wild thing" himself, he later created this enduring classic of children's literature.

One might also be inspired by a practical problem: Dr. Seuss, another children's writer, had no such dark experience; his classic writing stemmed from his annoyance that his children had nothing interesting or fun on which to practice their newly acquired reading skills. Inspiration comes in many forms; our inspirations, in part, shape the directions in which our minds flow.

What we experience is perhaps the most influential on the thought processes that affect the work we do with our minds. Our experiences are a huge part of who we are. The unique personality encapsulated in each mind influences what it does with its capabilities.

Experiences can include education or, unfortunately, lack thereof. With only a few exceptions, most great leaders in Western society have been male; this was simply because women tended to be educated less. Women who could read and write, or who were schooled in statecraft, for example, proved themselves to be just as capable of advanced and innovative thought as their male counterparts. Still, for every Anne Bradstreet, there were many more of her seventeenth-century contemporaries who did not get a chance to set their thoughts down as poetry. For every Queen Nefertiti bringing Egypt together, or Cleopatra, there were perhaps hundreds of women, or even more, who could have done the same or better given the chance, but the experiences they had did not allow it.

Another form of experience that is especially telling is experience with other people. Love and friendship have been inspirational for many artists, thinkers, and writers, both male and female. The experience of war inspired a whole generation after World War I, and many other experiences that people have with and of each other have had similar effects on individuals.

Our experiences are such a crucial part of who we are that it seems unlikely that any thinker would be able to separate his or her mind's work entirely from experiences. Today, thousands of young people around the world go off to college each year to experience the life of the mind and the training their brains will need to produce their future contributions. Without this experience, who would these young people become? The answer is hard to fathom, which puts into high relief just how important our experiences, educational and otherwise, are to the lives of our minds.

A final way that our minds are shaped is with eustress. This human factor has been defined in many ways but can be thought of as the set of positive, constructive responses to stress. The stressful activity that each person seeks out, be it running marathons, teaching classes, or performing difficult acrobatic tricks, causes a state or feeling of eustress; the pursuit of this positive feeling of challenge and excitement can influence our mind's work greatly.

Most people are unaware of the concept of eustress, but understanding it can truly provide insight into why people think, create, and interact as they do. Pursuing one's curiosity, even when the going gets tough, is the definition of eustress, and those in possession of great minds often do this. Anyone who loves a challenge experiences eustress; this experience is part of what pushes the great minds to think and act in particular ways. Thinkers, leaders, and other luminaries tend not to back away from challenges, but to enjoy the mental—and sometimes physical—exercise of taking them on.

The challenges that people in possession of great minds are most likely to undertake vary. Most intelligent and curious people enjoy taking on challenges they feel they can meet. However, the very difficulty of a challenge is part of its appeal. Such a challenge could be anything from teaching to climbing Mount Everest, but the important point is that the pursuit of eustress leads many people to take on the challenges they do.

Our minds are like muscles; we stretch them according to a variety of human factors, small and large that works together to make our minds unique. These factors also engender and pique curiosity so that the great minds of the world can continue forward, moving ever further into the realm of all there is to know.

Chapter Two

Although there are a myriad of human factors that affect the trajectory and the work of the mind, ultimately, the social factors stand out the most. We are, at heart, social beings; the high level of organization in our society is one of the things that make us, as humans, unique among all beings in the animal kingdom. It makes sense, then, that our socialization consequently affects every level of our interaction with others and our mind's work and functioning; it also influences - or even entirely changes the work we choose to do with our minds, or the challenges we choose to take on.

Education, whether a traditional Western education or one of some other paradigm, is of huge importance to the workings of the most advanced minds among us. With some few notable exceptions, great thinkers are educated; their minds are agile, moving from topic to topic with ease, and they have practice thinking about difficult, abstract ideas and concepts. It is no accident or coincidence that the people acknowledged to have some of the greatest minds in history are educated; in fact, education plays a crucial role in preparing the mind to do great work.

Educating the mind is more than the simple absorption of facts. In fact, education can change how a person reacts to challenges, synthesizes new information, and even—perhaps most intriguingly—how a person interacts with and reacts to other people. Coming across an intellectually superior person can be a stimulating experience that causes the mind to work hard to keep up, although interaction and conversation with an intellectual equal is likely to be beneficial and enjoyable to both people.

However, a mind that is less than equal to one's own, whether the inequality is due to innate intelligence differences, human factors, education, or some other source, will cause the educated mind to act differently. A reactive mind will instinctively know to slow down or repeat explanations, use different vocabulary, or otherwise adjust to the level of the person or persons in question.

Social interactions thus have much to do with the mind's behavior, since whom one interacts with, and on what level, is crucial in determining how quickly and how complexly the mind works. This can change from moment to moment, and even within subsequent interactions between the same two people. For example, the first time a student learns Einstein's theory of relativity, he or she may be confused and require the learned professor to slow down explanations and information to make the interaction productive. When, years later, the student returns as an expert on relativity, the professor's mind no doubt acts differently—and the student's, as well. Now, the two minds move at the same quick pace, working together to forge ahead.

Whether inside or outside of the classroom, this sort of social interaction changes how our minds work, sometimes from moment to moment. This is the secret to "think tanks" and other places where thought is created, sometimes at a dizzying pace; at a meeting of equal minds, none of the impediments exist that are created when unequal minds (be it on a single subject or overall) try to commune and interact. While all people must interact with others who are more curious, creative, and intelligent than they, and those who are less so, understanding how the mind reacts to these differences is key to a deep comprehension of the mind's inner workings.

Education can create great opportunities for the mind, and the lack of education, unfortunately, can keep these opportunities from presenting themselves. If everyone in the world were given rigorous education in the field that best suited his or her aptitude and choice, it is impossible to know how far we could have advanced scientifically and culturally, or in solving the world's problems. Unfortunately, the sad flip side of this truth is that untold potential is wasted, because some people have no access to education or equitable opportunity to exercise and grow their mental capacities and capabilities. From parts of the world where little education exists for anyone to countries where, for religious or cultural reasons, education is denied to women, people unlucky enough to be born there are not able to meet their intellectual potential. Inequality of opportunity is a huge social factor. Its influence on how the mind develops and works truly cannot be underestimated. Wherever people are too poor to afford education or are unable to pursue it for other reasons, opportunity to explore great ideas and make great advances may be lost, and we may never know it.

On the other hand, education and social norms can combine to make wonderful opportunities available for people to expand their minds. The great universities of the world, along with craftspeople and others who educate, provide wonderful opportunities to grow and change the mind. These range widely—from science to music to the pursuit of visual arts, literature, and much more. The curiosity of those who have educational opportunities reaches the furthest and is the most productive in terms of new discoveries and the creation of new ideas, works of art, and other items.

Besides education, relationships with others is a social factor that can influence the processes of the mind; it is a subcategory of experience. In fact, one could argue that the relationships people form are the ultimate human factor, helping them to broaden their horizons and thus change how their minds work, what they comprehend, and what they invent or think up.

A relationship with a beloved teacher or student, like that between Plato and Socrates can push both student and teacher to new heights of understanding and new intellectual feats. Because the relationship is a trusting one built over time, both student and teacher are free to explore new ideas.

Other kinds of relationships can be beneficial as well. Any businessperson knows the value of networking for career advancement; any new acquaintance might be the key to a new job or opportunity. The same general idea holds true in the development of the life of the mind: new people can open up new horizons and provide new opportunities, whether they are found in one's new school, on a trip, or simply through sharing a book or experiencing art with someone.

However, forming new relationships is not the only important thing; so are the depth and variety of relationships. If one has experience with all different types of people, really getting to know them and their perspectives and cultures, the more likely one can assimilate such influences into one's own mental framework. This can make for a richer personal perspective and perhaps, better ideas or creations. Belief systems may hold some people back from forming relationships with those very different from themselves but connecting with others is beneficial. Think of Marc Antony without the influences of both Cleopatra and Julius Caesar, or of the way that Franklin D. Roosevelt could negotiate not just with allies, but with enemies, in the formation of the United Nations. Without the ability to form relationships open-mindedly with a variety of different people, the United Nations could never have been formed, nor could it have survived to the present day as a force for good in the world.

Productivity is another social factor that influences mental acuity and activity. Too much going on in one's life can be catastrophic to being mentally productive. Anything that affects productivity can be a problem. To see this, one has only to think of Sylvia Plath, whose marriage was part of what drove her to suicide. While it may have inspired some of her poetry, it also contributed to paralyzing her and caused her to end her life far too prematurely. Her productivity was direly affected by the people around her.

Productivity can also be affected simply because one has too much on one's mind—due, perhaps, to responsibilities to others. Such thoughts might include how to provide for one's family or afford medicine for a sick child, or simply how to make time for all the nagging concerns that come with relationships, parenthood, or any close interaction. With all of these thoughts crowding one's head, it is hard to think of the life of the mind and to engage in intellectual pursuits, even if one wants to.

Productivity can be increased by dint of practice and education. These social factors of mental activity can be a repeating circle, a kind of self-fulfilling prophecy. Those who have the time, mental space, and energy to productively engage in the life of the mind are in turn more likely to be able to do so again and more often, because they have practiced and acquired the habit of complex thought. Those who are never able to engage in mental gymnastics, or even daydreaming, are always working on something else they see as more important, for whatever reason. Important as mundane concerns undoubtedly are, it cannot but be acknowledged that our productivity as a society suffers because not all of its members are free to be productive thinkers. Instead, many must fight against the day-to-day realities of life, which keeps them from thinking creatively, and perhaps, from becoming the curious thinkers they could be.

Another social factor that affects mental processes is dependability. Some people really like a schedule they can count on daily—an unchanging list of times at which they do certain things. Many successful authors, for example, must write at certain times of the day to get anything done, and other people believe that they do their best work at a certain time, be it early in the morning or late at night. Some people take on professions that provide mental work at certain times of day. Teachers, for example, often tend to be "morning people" who are at their best long before others are awake. Orchestra conductors, who must lead large groups in artistic expression, are often creatures of the evening, not even beginning their work until late in the day and often going on into the wee hours of the morning.

Having a dependable schedule is not only important for those who work best at certain times of day; genius may strike at any moment, but most people are more likely to be productive over the course of a long period if they are given some structure—whether they give it to themselves or it is imposed upon them. Publication deadlines function this way; they force authors to get their ideas into a readable form by a certain date. Without such dependability, some people might never be able to marshal their ideas.

This is especially true of perfectionists, who, without deadlines, might feel compelled to continue refining their ideas or work, never allowing them to see the light of day. Having a dependable schedule makes people like this more likely to be able to share their ideas with the world.

Dependability is also a trait that can come with practice: writers write more easily, painters paint more easily, and musicians play better when they continue to practice. Completing practice allows anyone, from athletes to chess players, to get better at what they do. The maxim that "practice makes perfect" is certainly the truth in any kind of mental exercise. The more one does, over and over, whatever one wishes to be good at, the easier it becomes and the better one is at it. While the average person will not, perhaps, see practice sketches or bits of music that never become publishable, they are being made, day in and day out. Those who produce them are working dependably to get better at the amazing feats they do with their minds.

Genius may come in bursts, but the truly productive mind works over a period of time. Of course, a few minds are well known for a single achievement that may have come in a moment, perhaps, of clarity or excitement. Harper Lee's *To Kill a Mockingbird* is a classic novel read in schools around the world; it is a paean to social justice that contains one of the best heroes of all time: the righteous lawyer, Atticus Finch. Perhaps Lee had nothing else to say, or perhaps she was never able to marshal her considerable talents toward another novel; either way, she never published anything else. Had Lee written more, she might be considered even greater by history; instead, her literary merit is judged on just one novel. Other writers, whose individual novels might not compare favorably with *To Kill a Mockingbird*, may come to mind more quickly simply because they have written more.

While individual ideas or work may be brilliant, society hails those thinkers, leaders, and doers with staying power as our best. Being president of the United States is not something one does for a moment, or even a month or year; being able to sustain excellence is the sign of a disciplined and hardworking mind at its fullest potential, taking on challenges and working through them. In his current term, President Obama has been faced with expected and unexpected challenges, from moving soldiers out of Iraq as promised to dealing with the sudden shooting in Newtown, Connecticut, unable to go to his daughter's scheduled dance recital.

The way to true excellence is sustained work, moving smoothly from one challenge to the next, taking on and excelling in multiple roles. This is a social factor, because each different challenge, from a diplomatic meeting to consoling the nation through a tragedy—involves working with people. Being able to sustain this work and do it with precision, quality, and heart at all times is a special thing. This is the mind-set that our greatest leaders have, and this factor—the way they relate with others sustainably—can truly set them apart.

Chapter Three

The mind does not work in a vacuum.
As we have seen, internal factors, such as our
beliefs and experiences, can have a lot to do
with what we choose to work on and how we
think; our minds are also influenced by social
factors, from our schedules to the people we
meet and the relationships we build. These are
not the only factors that influence how the mind
works, however.

The world is full of things we want;
indeed, having wants as well as needs is a
hallmark of the human condition. Ambition and
greed, whether for money, prestige, status,
renown, or something else, all affect how the

mind works. These motivations can change our emotions, causing interference in the mind's work. Although emotions are an important part of any mental endeavor or creative exercise, certain kinds can cause distraction. When emotional wants, such as financial inducements get to be too much, they can get in the way of productive mental work and of the emotions that spearheaded the challenge in the first place, forcing productivity to a halt.

Human and social factors may have an effect upon what a mind can come up with and how much product it can put out, be it ideas, creative writing, or something else. But functional factors that come from the outside world—things that keep the mind from working to its potential or keep it working at its best—

are important too and must be explored if we are

to truly understand how the best minds work

what can seem, from the outside, almost to be

magic.

One functional concern of the great mind

is how to implement ideas. The most fantastical

inventions, or the most complete and wonderful

solutions that might hypothetically cure

diseases, are truly of no use if they cannot be

implemented and made real. Some people excel

at finding creative solutions or thinking of new

things but cannot fit them to actuality. The

fascinating world of fashion design can offer

some examples. Couture fashion is often

completely un-wearable; a beautiful dress by

Saint Laurent or Givenchy is only useful to the extent that it can be worn. When even models, who are in the profession of wearing clothes, cannot wear them, the clothes may be beautiful, but they are not useful; thus, their importance to the world is limited and the contribution of the designer is less, in this case, than of someone who makes something both beautiful *and* wearable.

Implementation is a challenge for great minds throughout the disciplines. To return to the example of President Obama: He has many good ideas about how to solve the problems that plague the United States of America, from the issue of debt to health insurance reform, changes to immigration laws, and gun control statutes—as do the lawmakers around him. However, because of the current, extremely partisan political situation in Congress, few reforms are actually being enacted. It is difficult to get anything done, it seems, and therefore, even the best ideas of Obama and others are of limited utility. Thus, history may see them as simply ideas, not effective actions. It is not the minds of Obama or of any of the lawmakers that are at fault here; it is merely the functional reality that their ideas are being blocked from being put into practice.

Implementing ideas can be physically difficult, as well. Copernicus was an amazing astronomer in his time, but many of his ideas were never able to be proven or worked through, simply because the technology to view the parts of the skies that he needed to see did not yet exist. Sometimes, time and technology cause a functional barrier to implementing even the best ideas, and this problem cannot be underestimated. If Steve Jobs, founder and visionary of the Apple brand, had lived in another century, surely he would still have had great ideas, but some of his particular genius could not have been implemented, simply because the technology did not exist then. There were likely many inventors who visualized such things as airplanes long before the technology became available to build them, but it fell to Orville and Wilbur Wright, who happened to come along at the right moment in history.

The ability to implement ideas is a huge functional issue, for better or worse. To find the greatest success, the person who has the ideas does not necessarily need to be able to implement them him or herself, but if nobody else can—whether the technology does not exist or there is some other barrier—the problem can keep even the most fulfilled, curious, well-educated, and disciplined mind from being able to do its best possible work.

Focus definitely helps great minds reach their potential. Focusing on a specific goal, drive, and determination have been shown, both anecdotally and by scientific study, to make the difference between success and failure. Scientists try, over and over again, to get the results they seek. For example, drug researchers might tweak their formula tens of times, each tweak necessitating its own round of tests and research, simply to find the right formula to cure a disease or fix a problem. Their single-minded focus on the goal is commendable; it allows them to eventually find the right formula and, by dint of never giving up, to improve the fortunes of humanity.

However, sometimes long-term focus can be too single-minded. Sometimes an unsolvable problem should be laid aside, rather than allowing it to consume one's mental energy. Some great minds have driven themselves insane over the centuries, contemplating questions – at times with no answer. Overly single-minded focus can have more concrete negative effects, as well. In the mid-twentieth century, scientists at the Tuskegee Institute were so focused on finding a cure for syphilis that they infected unsuspecting people and did not cure them, but allowed them to suffer. They were so focused on the end result that they decided that individual people did not matter, especially since the social mores of the time dictated that their subjects, who were African-American and mostly poor, were second-class citizens at best. This kind of focus led to staggeringly tragic ethical violations, as hundreds of people died in pain simply because the scientists had designed a completely morally corrupt experiment to gain scientific knowledge.

Long-term focus can be both good and bad. Focus can definitely allow one to persevere through setbacks to do important things and make beneficial discoveries. However, too much single-mindedness can consume minds and cause people to make ethically suspect decisions; that way, it can even cancel out the positive side of any discoveries.

In addition, whether or not the intense work of the mind comes to fruition can depend on its costs. Of course, lack of money has stopped many people from bringing their exciting, creative, innovative dreams to life. However, there can also be hidden costs: functional barriers to true creative and intellectual innovation.

The pressure of sustained and difficult work of any kind can be problematic for health. Presidents of the United States seem to age radically in their four- or eight-year terms; nearly all come out with gray hair and looking far older than they did when they went in. This is probably due to the constant stress they are under in their work as the functional leaders of the free world, no matter when in history they serve. However, health consequences can be much direr than this. Stress can contribute to high blood pressure, stroke, and heart attack. Many great thinkers have been cut down in their prime. Stephen Hawking, an amazing physicist, has come up with brilliant theorems and ideas about the way the universe functions, yet has done all of this while unable to speak or move due to amyotrophic lateral sclerosis (ALS), a disease that has stolen his ability to take care of himself. How much more could he have accomplished if he did not have this overwhelming health challenge and concern? We will never know.

Another type of cost or pressure that often impedes the work of the mind is the fact that the work itself often impedes the lifestyle one would like to live, putting pressure on family relationships and even precluding them, in some cases. Almost everyone has experienced a time when work got in the way of family fun or bonding, or kept one from working out, cooking healthy food, making religious observance, or something else important. The life of the mind can definitely get in the way. "Workaholics" avoid the problem by making their work their lifestyle; they make sure that work comes first and therefore minimize pressure on lifestyle. However, these people may not have as fulfilling lives as those who live with more balance.

Happiness, in general, is subject to pressure from intensive mental work. What constitutes happiness, of course, is different for each individual. Perhaps those who find deep personal satisfaction and fulfillment in their work are the happiest: they do not find that their work costs them happiness, but rather that the intensity of work adds to it. Not all great

thinkers and leaders are wired this way, though,

and the problem of the unhappy genius can be

seen again and again.

A final functional issue that can keep

one from truly reaching the limits of one's

genius is the limitation of one's own scope of

ideas. Like so many of the other factors

explored in this book, this is partly a result of

one's education and the ideas and beliefs to

which one is exposed. Genius may be limited by

what a person can conceive: if one cannot

visualize the atom, for example, there is no way

that one can achieve an understanding of ions,

or of technology such as the electron

microscope. We are limited, in general, by the

times in which we live: no doubt, two hundred years from now, we will have solved the fuel crisis with types of power that have not even been invented yet and that scientists today can only barely see on the horizon, no matter how well educated and forward thinking they may be.

There are limits to the questions and curiosities a normal mind explores. They are bound by the time in which one lives, one's interests and education level, and a myriad of other factors, such as the amount of time someone has to devote to philosophical or creative inquiry or work—even a person's facility with language (or with the language of a given discipline). Many functional and successful people are simply not disposed to be curious or to engage in intellectual exercises. Others have many admirable qualities and are successful at what their careers or lives demand, but they may not be good leaders or have any desire to be. Still others who might have become good leaders never get into a situation that demands they develop such a capacity. This is not to say that these people are bad or in any way inferior to those whose curiosity leads them to become great minds in their own time and beyond. Rather, they are merely differently limited: the scope of their mind's eye does not allow for high-level creative or intellectual work.

Even the most creative and brilliant people are limited in scope to some extent: there never has been a single person who could excel in all disciplines, let alone innovate in all areas. Some people are simply not talented in some disciplines. Not all of us have the physical build to be football players, for instance—and of those who do, not all have the mental discipline to memorize plays or the mental acuity to visualize them, or to understand how to execute them at a moment's notice. Brilliant people may be great at what they do and in terms of IQ and other measures of intelligence, but each is limited in what he or she can conceive of, work on, and accomplish. These limitations come from both circumstance and the way brains develop; we have no control over either. Though limitations in scope and curiosity are not necessarily tragic or even undesirable, they should be acknowledged and understood by those seeking to understand the way the mind works.

Chapter Four

Many people have great thoughts, but
the ability of others to understand them makes a
difference in whether the ideas will live on in
posterity or be lost forever with the death of the
thinker. The way we communicate our ideas is
crucial for its usefulness; some people have a
facility with communication that sets them apart
from others whose ideas are just as good but are
unable to get them across and make them clear
to others. Ideas must be understood when
shared; eventually, they may even be improved
upon and can inspire others down the road.

Cooperative communication in different
settings can definitely have an impact on one's

ideas, and how one expresses them can also have an impact on how they are received. At a meeting or in the classroom, a truly advanced mind may need to adopt strategies so that he or she can be understood; not knowing these strategies, or not seeing the signs that they are needed — such as a listener looking confused can be a definite problem for even the smartest person. In a meeting or classroom setting, when the goal is to explain one's views to another person or people who probably don't understand the topic as well as the expert at the front of the room, it is necessary to tailor one's communication style. One must emphasize the important points, slow the pace, repeat, and even leave out parts or simplify vocabulary or concepts, if needed.

When one's audience is likely to have a background in the subject and can follow the language of its discourse with relative ease such as a scientist at a scientific conference, these experts can speak freely without modifying their communication style. Where many great thinkers run into trouble, however, is making sure that they can be understood when they step out of their disciplines. A great scientist who can bring down the house at a conference of peers is not necessarily the one to give a toast at a wedding; he might be hard to understand, or simply boring or awkward. Different events and circumstances call for different modes of communication, and creative or intellectual work can be hampered when someone lacks an understanding of how to communicate.

The importance of communication can truly not be overestimated; world leaders have to work together in the delicate work of diplomacy, and they must contend not only with differing cultural norms of communication and different personal styles, but with language barriers as well. Communication can be its own special genius; people can be amazingly skilled at communicating the messages of others. But any impressive mind-work or other form of contribution demands some modicum of communication skills, without exception, so that the ideas can be communicated or so that diplomacy can be conducted.

Perhaps the most important part of understanding the amazing work our minds can do is understanding more about communication and the mind's role in deciding what mode of it is best to get ideas across and make them understood. Socioeconomic concerns, education, and culture all influence communication, so understanding them all is important if one wants to understand the mind, its function, and its work.

People have different approaches to problem solving, which is good, because when we work in groups, the diversity of thought processes, philosophies, schools of thought, and approaches to tasks allows us to choose among approaches and can accelerate problem solving. Collaboration can be a richer experience, regardless of the outcome. However, the particular approach any given person might take is worth exploring, simply to understand how a mind truly works.

Approaches to thinking are often divided into the two general categories of the analytical and the intuitive. Those who use the intuitive approach might be thought of as guessing, or, perhaps more accurately, feeling their way through a problem. People who do this often have high emotional intelligence quotients— they understand others and are able to empathize, putting themselves in others' shoes when they solve problems or approach challenges. Those of this persuasion may just be that way naturally; many people just approach things from an emotional, intuitive perspective. But it is also possible that they approach problems this way, via "guessing," if you will, because they were never taught to think logically. This is not to say that people who approach thought like this are unintelligent. Rather, some of them did not have practice in critical thinking or framing their thoughts in cohesive ways in their early life. As we have seen, education and acculturation, among other influences, shape the way we think.

Without rigorous education that prioritizes questioning and solving problems rather than just memorization, and that rewards true understanding rather than simple recall, people might well never really learn how to think, through no fault of their own. In China, for example, students are expected to memorize and parrot much more than American students, and they are not expected to seek out their own solutions or learn by doing. As a result, not all of the students in that system learn to think critically. Unfortunately, some people do not learn critical thinking because of income level— those who have to concentrate on work simply to survive or who do not have access to good teaching materials or teachers because of where they live are also less likely to be exposed to the

rigors or the discipline of critical thinking
coursework.

Just as intuitively "guessing" to solve
problems is natural to some, being analytical is
natural for others. Some people are just
naturally able to think in an organized fashion or
to reason through problems critically, despite
never having been taught logic. This is likely to
have been true throughout human history;
although the human ancestor who discovered
fire might have done so by accident, it would
take an analytical and careful mind to figure out
how best to use it and to discover agriculture
and other innovations that kept the race alive.
However, we are not all born with analytical
thinking, but it can be taught if one's cultural

and economic position allows for the quality and mode of schooling offering such instruction.

Which of these two modes of thinking is more likely to lead to truly innovative thought? Since the world certainly needs thinkers on both sides of this binary to contribute their best, we cannot choose one over the other. Those on the intuitive, emotional side of things may be better at understanding other people than an analytical person, but the analytical thinkers might be better suited to math research or to work in a lab, since such work requires strongly organized and logical thought.

The best thinkers for some pursuits may be somewhere in the middle of the spectrum, which is where most people are. Indeed, a healthy mix of intuitive and analytical thought may be what the best minds among us possess, and this is a good thing. Intuitive thought may come more naturally to some than others, but analytical thought can be taught; if our schools teach the next generation of thinkers strong analytical skills, we may end up with more people who can do both and who can become the best possible sorts of thinkers. This is one of the greatest reasons that the educational system, not just in the Western countries but worldwide, needs improvement: so that the next generation of thinkers is set up for success.

One of the best things to push a creative and intellectual mind into new heights of thought and exploration is interaction with other minds, both similar and dissimilar. Being exposed to intellectual and creative equals can be exciting and stimulating. Imagine a child with a rare disability who attends a convention of others who struggle with the same problems, have the same challenges, and look the same as he or she does. Suddenly, this child's outlook is transformed: these people already understand fundamental things about the child and his or her life. Something similar happens with creative minds when they are able to meet with others who are on the same level. Without the need to explain basic concepts or to dumb down or simplify their thoughts, the most intelligent and creative people among us can be inspired and stimulated by conversation and working with other creative minds. On the other hand, any mind can be inspired and pushed to new heights by interacting with others people who might be more intelligent or creative; they can learn of new ideas and find inspiration to stretch themselves.

Both of these processes take place at the great universities of the world—this is just one reason that the college and university system is so important for sustaining really innovative and interesting creative and intellectual endeavor. Bringing intelligent, driven people together is one of the best ways to stimulate the creation of new ideas and the shifting of paradigms. Even if everyone is not on the exact same level— perhaps especially if they are not—they can work together and inspire each other. It is

crucial for any intellectual or creative person to

experience a community of learners who are all

engaged in the life of the mind, whether it

comes at a convention, a conference, a writer's

retreat, or merely in their dormitory at university

or in a classroom or lab.

These experiences are truly

irreplaceable, and while not every creative or

analytical genius mentioned in these pages had

these experiences in a way we might be able to

replicate today, still they are likely to have

benefited at some point from intellectual and

creative discourse with others, whether teachers,

families, or friends. From family dinners around

the Mozart family's table, which would have

included more than ten high-level composers and musicians — to the Parisian salons of the eighteenth and nineteenth centuries, where philosophers, authors, artists, and thinkers met and mingled, the interaction of creative and curious minds with others that are equally creative and curious has been an important part of the development of genius in any field.

Interaction between and among those with creative minds can push everyone involved to new heights, but what about those who do their best work on their own? Author J.D. Salinger, who wrote the classic *Catcher in the Rye*, lived a solitary life to the point of being a recluse, losing his relationships with others—including his own children—since his need to be alone was so all-consuming. Ludwig van Beethoven, also a creative genius, spent more and more time alone, especially as his hearing receded, and there are countless other examples in all fields of those who did their best thinking and made their greatest contributions when they were by themselves. However, these may be more the exception than the rule.

This is not to denigrate the contributions of such amazing thinkers. Nor is it to say that being by oneself does not allow for any positive development—in fact, journaling, reflection, meditation, and simply enjoying solo activities or one's own company has been a refuge for great men and women, just as it is for regular people. This is true even for those who work with others daily, such as diplomat Condoleezza Rice: playing piano is her outlet. Working alone or being by oneself to reflect is an important part of the creative or the working process for many, and it should not be avoided or discounted. Overall, though, humans are social creatures, so it stands to reason that being together is good for people. Perhaps it is even more true for creative and intellectual individuals, who can work together and be inspired by each other to bring further advancement to society's collective thought and knowledge, changing the world as we know it for good, and mostly for the better.

Ultimately, who are we? What do the workings of each unique mind have to do with personality and with the contributions each

person makes to society, and how much of our

experiences are actually related to the people

we've met, experiences we have, our education,

or other social factors? Both human and social

factors, as well as how we communicate and

how we interact with each other, play into the

experience of any one person, including the

intellectual and creative worlds. As we have

seen, social factors are extremely powerful—

perhaps even more than people realize. One's

education, one's beliefs and one's environments

are all powerful determinants of the life of the

mind in each person.

Every person is capable of unique flights

of fancy. Some can do more than just imagine;

they can lead others, create beautiful works of art, and inspire people to change, or advance our understanding of the world. All of these people are creative and have imaginative minds, be they more analytical or more emotional, well educated, or self-taught.

Understanding our own mind is one of the hardest tasks we must undertake, yet also one of the most important. Knowing how our mind work allows us to use them to the best possible advantage, letting each of us explore more, reach a higher level of achievement in whatever we are passionate about and even contribute more to the world, whether creatively, intellectually, or both.

We are all innately curious. But how we harness and manage our curiosity depends on a wide variety of factors. Understanding them and how each of them might relate to our own unique situations and lives is the work of a lifetime, but ultimately, we must remember that who we are is due to the almost magical workings of the human mind. In the end, we are just characters within our own thoughts; only by stepping outside our imaginations and looking at ourselves analytically can we begin to better understand the curiosities that lie within our mind. Understanding our curiosities and what drives us is the first step in the long process of improving our world, each mind working individually and together with others to push

ever forward, into the new.

Made in the USA
Lexington, KY
08 October 2016